VINTAGE R🌀SE
MYSTERIES

CALL WAITING

EVAN JACOBS

VINTAGE ROSE
MYSTERIES

SADDLEBACK
EDUCATIONAL PUBLISHING
www.sdlback.com

ISBN: 978-1-68021-762-9
eBook: 978-1-64598-069-8

Printed in Malaysia
27 26 25 24 23   3 4 5 6 7

THE HISTORY OF THE VINTAGE ROSE ANTIQUE SHOP

The story begins with a sorcerer named Ervin Legend. He had a talent for making money. While traveling, Ervin bought items all over the world. He would have called himself a collector. Others might say hoarder. Once he grew tired of things, he sold them for a profit. "One man's junk is another man's treasure," he used to say.

Eventually, Ervin wanted to settle down. His home was in Scarecrow, California. But he needed somewhere to put all of his things. Ervin opened the Vintage Rose Antique Shop in 1912. It was a place to keep his collections. His wife, Visalia, inspired the shop's name. She loved roses and kept them in vases all over the shop. "Roses mask the smell of old things," she would say.

After the shop opened, Ervin kept traveling. He collected pieces to sell from all over. In 1949, Ervin and Visalia went to Cairo, Egypt. While there, the couple disappeared. Nobody knows what happened to them. Some say Ervin's love of sorcery might have been to blame. He may have looked into something he shouldn't have.

Family members took over the shop. None were quite like Ervin, though. Without his passion, the business began to fail. His sister believed it was cursed.

In 1979, the Legends put the shop up for sale. Rose Myers bought it. She was odd, like Ervin. Her passion for old things was like his. "Everything has a story," she would say, with a twinkle in her eye. From a young age, Rose had looked for bargains. She would resell things for a profit. Buying the Vintage Rose was her dream come true. The place was old. It was filled with odd treasures. Plus, Rose was part of the name of the store. It seemed like this was meant to be.

Rose ran the shop for 40 years. When she passed away, it closed. The business had been left to her nephew, Evan Stewart. He was Rose's closest living relative. The Stewart family moved to Scarecrow. They reopened the shop in 2019.

Today, the shop still holds many treasures. Collectors come from all over. Some have purchased these mysterious relics. Are they magical? Do they watch over the store? We may never find out. Or will we?

CHAPTER 1

RING, RING

Tenley looks up at the ceiling. "It's weird that we can't hear the rain down here," she says.

"Well," I say. "We *are* underground."

She smiles. "You're right, smart guy."

Tenley and I are in the basement of her parents' store, the Vintage Rose Antique Shop. We're supposed to be organizing it. I had no idea how much stuff was down here, though. Now I'm starting to regret volunteering to help.

"Tenley," I say, picking up a board game that is definitely older than me. "Where did all this junk come from?"

She sighs. "My dad's Aunt Rose. She owned this place and left it to us when she died. That's why we moved to Scarecrow, remember? Anyway, I think my great aunt was a hoarder."

"What makes you think that?" I laugh.

We both look around the basement. This place is

textbook creepy. There's a creaky staircase leading down to it. The only light comes from a bare bulb in the ceiling. You have to pull a string to turn it on. Furniture and stacks of old boxes cover the floor. Ancient toys and books line the shelves. Cobwebs hang off everything.

The weirdest part is the smell. I swear the whole place smells like dead roses, even upstairs.

"We don't have to finish today, Ryan," Tenley says. "My parents just want us to start organizing this stuff. They keep getting new things to sell all the time. The store is getting crowded."

"It seems past crowded. So . . . where do we start?"

Tenley walks over to some metal shelves at the back of the room. They are filled with cleaning supplies. She pulls out two pairs of yellow rubber gloves.

"We should wear these," she says, tossing a pair of gloves to me. "I've seen rats down here."

"Oh, great," I mumble, starting to move boxes.

We begin to organize the mess. It's not really clear what we're doing. Tenley seems to be moving everything to the middle of the basement. I follow her lead.

After a few minutes, we're sweating. The rain has made it musty down here. I wipe my forehead with my sleeve.

Tenley pulls off her sweatshirt. It's red and says

Scarecrow Middle School on it. That's where we go. My friend Jen introduced us there last year. When Tenley first came to our school, Jen was her class buddy. For a while, the three of us hung out together. But we haven't seen Jen much lately.

"You think Jen misses us?" Tenley asks.

A chill runs down my spine. Not only are we in a spooky basement, but it seems like Tenley is reading my mind.

"She'll come back," I say. "Jen just got busy. That happens with her sometimes."

"Whatever."

Tenley thinks Jen dropped us on purpose. She's still bummed about it.

All I know is that Jen got really into ballet. Her big sister was taking classes, so Jen started going too. She has class every day after school now. Tenley thinks it's an unhealthy obsession.

"Thanks for helping me today," Tenley says. "I'd never be able to do all this on my own."

"No problem," I say. "We were going to hang out anyway. And where else would I be able to find a knitted toilet paper cover?"

Tenley laughs as I hold up the pink cylinder made of yarn.

"Plus, you'll be done quicker if I help."

"That's the truth," she says.

Ring! Ring!

A phone is ringing. It's not one of ours, though. This sounds like an old-fashioned phone.

Tenley and I look at each other.

"Did you change your ringtone?" she asks.

"No. Do your parents have an old phone down here?"

Tenley shakes her head. Her expression changes. She looks nervous.

The ringing continues.

I walk around the basement, trying to figure out where the ringing is coming from. As I get closer to the back wall, it gets louder. A black curtain hangs over the wall. Strange symbols are painted on the curtain in white.

"Don't move that—," Tenley starts.

Her warning is too late. I've already pulled back the curtain. Behind it, there's a door with a huge padlock on it.

Ring! Ring!

I look down and see an old black phone on the ground. It looks like the type of phone I've seen in black-and-white TV shows. A silver dial catches the light. White numbers form a circle on it and go from one to nine. There's a zero after the nine too. On top, there's a handset.

The phone continues to ring.

CHAPTER 2

"I'M HOME"

Should I answer it?" I ask.

"No," Tenley says. "I've never seen that thing before." There is no smile on her face. She seems genuinely scared.

"Why can't I pick it up?"

"Because . . ." Tenley looks at the phone. She seems transfixed. "I said not to."

The ringing continues. We stare at the phone. It feels like this goes on forever.

After a few minutes, I look at Tenley and smile slightly. My friend can get overly serious sometimes. But usually I can make her laugh.

An idea comes to me.

I pick up the phone.

"Ryan!" Tenley scowls at me. "I said *no!*"

I put the receiver to my ear.

"Hello?" I squawk in a high-pitched voice. This is

my impression of Lucy from *Lucy Loudmouth*. It's one of Tenley's favorite shows.

"Hi, toots!" a voice says loudly. We can both hear it through the receiver. "I'm home to see you!"

"Hang up," Tenley whispers. Then she grabs the receiver out of my hand and puts it back on the cradle.

"I told you not to answer it, Ryan!"

Suddenly, we hear a creaking noise. It's coming from the stairs. Heavy footsteps move down them.

Fear rises in my throat. Who's coming down to the basement?

We turn around to look.

It's just Jay, Tenley's brother. His face is glued to his phone as he walks down the stairs. He stops on the last step.

"This place is still a mess," Jay says, looking around. "Why?"

"We're working on it!" Tenley snaps. "You're not our boss."

"Actually, Mom and Dad just left. When they're gone, I *am* the boss."

"Oh, big whoop!" Tenley says. "What are you going to do? Fire us?"

"Just get back to work," Jay says. "You're not getting paid to mess around."

He starts walking back up the stairs.

"Wait," I call after him. "We're getting paid?"

He turns and looks at me. "You? Sorry, no. Twig gets an allowance. She can pay you if she wants."

Tenley rolls her eyes. Her brother loves to tease her with that nickname. "Let's finish organizing this place," she says. "Then we can get out of here."

I help Tenley stack more boxes in the middle of the basement. Neither of us says anything.

"So who do you think that was on the phone?" I finally ask.

Tenley doesn't respond. It's clear she doesn't want to talk about it.

Secretly, I hope the phone will ring again. Even though it's weird, I think it's kind of cool too.

We continue to organize for the rest of the afternoon, but the phone stays silent.

Later, I'm walking home. Luckily the rain has stopped. The wind is picking up, though. It's getting dark too. I zip my coat and shove my hands in my pockets.

Tenley asked if I wanted her mom to drive me home. I chose to walk. Some people my age don't like being out when it gets dark. It doesn't bother me. What is there to be afraid of? In some ways, the town is more peaceful in the dark. The way the streetlights reflect off the puddles is pretty.

It's a lot colder now. I should have worn gloves and a hat. Rumor has it there's a big storm moving toward Scarecrow. My mom said it could be the worst one in 75 years.

I don't believe it. Weather predictions are never right. The storm won't be that bad. People love to worry about stuff like this, though. It gives them something to do.

All I hope is that the internet doesn't go out. That happened once during a storm. At school, we had to use our textbooks instead of our tablets for the whole day. My parents said that's what they always did in school. It must have been so boring.

On my walk, I pass a small row of shops. There's a pay phone at the end of them. I've never noticed it before. The black receiver rests on a silver cradle. Having a pay phone here is so odd. Why would anybody use one nowadays? Everyone has cell phones.

Suddenly, the phone starts to ring.

I stop and stare at it.

What are the odds that I would hear two ancient phones ringing in one day?

I decide not to answer this one.

CHAPTER 3

FAMOUS LAST WORDS

Do you want your fries?" I ask.

Tenley and I are eating lunch. The cafeteria at Scarecrow Middle School is full of students. Nobody wants to go outside because it's cold and windy. I guess the storm is moving in.

"No, you can have them." She pushes a small cardboard tray of potato wedges toward me.

"Thanks."

We both have our phones out. Lunch is when we check Instagram and share memes. I just sent Tenley a funny video of a dog and cat playing piano together.

"Did that guy ever call back yesterday?" I ask. For some reason, I've been thinking about the phone in the Vintage Rose basement. It was so weird that it rang out of nowhere.

"No," Tenley says. "I didn't go back down there after you left."

"Oh," I say, putting a fry in my mouth. "Do you think that phone can call out?"

"I don't know. Who cares, though? It's just an old phone. We have better ones." Tenley holds up her smartphone.

"Maybe we should try it," I say, smiling.

"No."

"Come on. It might be fun."

"I've told you how weird that basement is. Besides, that phone appeared right in front of the secret room. You know—the one I never open because of what happened? With the doll?"

A few months back, Tenley told me about a doll. She found it in a secret room in the basement of the Vintage Rose. The room was locked, but Tenley opened it. Then the doll got out and caused all kinds of problems. Apparently, it tried to hurt Tenley and her family.

When she told me the story, I thought Tenley was just trying to scare me. It all seemed impossible. Horror movies might have creepy dolls in them, but they're not real. No doll I've ever seen can walk around and hurt people.

"I know about the doll," I say. "This isn't a doll, though. It's just a phone. And it wasn't in the locked room, remember? Let's try it once. Maybe it'll be fun."

CHAPTER 4

HOME AGAIN

Tenley holds up her index finger. "One call out," she says. "Then we're done. Being down here gives me the creeps."

We're back in the basement. I'm holding the phone. The smell of dead roses doesn't seem as strong as it did yesterday. It was drizzling a bit when we got to the shop. Maybe that takes away the smell. Dampness should make it worse, though. My nose must be getting used to it.

"What number should I call?" I ask.

Tenley shrugs. "I don't know. Try calling your phone."

I put my finger in the hole next to the five. Then I turn the silver dial. For each number, I do the same. It takes forever to dial my whole number.

"I can't believe this is how phones used to work," I say.

Finally, I finish dialing and hold the receiver up

to my ear. Tenley and I listen for my phone to start ringing. Nothing happens.

"I guess it doesn't work," she says.

"Bummer. Can I try one more time?"

"No!"

Tenley grabs the receiver and puts it back on the cradle.

All of a sudden, the phone rings.

We look at each other. I giggle. She doesn't smile at all.

"Well, it's working," I say. "Answer it."

"No way. Just put it back where you found it. Let's get out of here."

"Tenley, somebody's calling your parents' business."

"So? My parents can answer it then."

I pick up the receiver. Tenley shoots me an angry look.

"Lorraine? I said I'm home to see you, toots!" a man's voice says. It's the same man who called yesterday. He doesn't sound as happy now.

"Why'd you hang up last time?" he asks. "It's pouring out here. I just got off my ship."

"I'm sorry," I say, looking at Tenley. Her face is

filled with terror. I smile at her. A wrong number is no big deal. "I don't think you're home to see *me*, sir."

"Who is this?" The man's tone is much angrier now. "Why are you playing games with my phone? Put Lorraine on. *Now!*"

"Um," I mumble, trying not to crack up. "Lorraine's not here, sir."

My friends and I have made some prank calls. I'm used to hearing a grumpy voice on the other end of the phone. But we didn't call this guy. This is like a prank call in reverse.

"You're going to get it for messin' with this phone call! I've been at sea a long time. We just got through one of the worst storms in history. Our boat almost capsized. You have no right to mess with my phone call. Now put Lorraine on!"

Tenley glares at me. She looks more upset than the man on the phone sounds. Before I can say anything else, she rips the receiver out of my hand and slams it down on the cradle.

CHAPTER 5

UNPLUGGED

Ryan!" Tenley growls through gritted teeth.

"What are you mad at me for?" I can't help but laugh. That only makes Tenley angrier.

"I warned you about this basement. You promised you would only try *one* call."

"All I did was answer a phone!"

Slowly, I realize maybe this situation isn't so funny. The man on the phone sounded very angry. He said he was going to get me. Still, there's no way he could find us. At least, I don't think there is.

Tenley puts the old phone back on the ground.

"Let's get out of here." She walks toward the stairs.

"Are you sure you've never heard it ring before?" I ask, following her.

"For the millionth time," she says. "I never saw the thing until yesterday. Honestly, it's like it just showed up out of nowhere."

17

"That's strange," I say, eyeing the phone's gray cord. It's attached to the back of it.

"What are you looking at?" Tenley asks. She stands on the first step of the staircase.

"I'm seeing where the cord goes." I walk back to the phone and begin following the cable along the wall.

"Why?" she snaps. "What does that matter?"

"Maybe somebody just plugged it in. That could be why you never noticed it before."

"Following the cord isn't going to tell you that."

"I know, but maybe there's a clue where it's plugged in."

"Ryan," Tenley sighs. Her tone is exasperated. "Let's go. There's no need to spend any more time down here."

The cord goes under a small workbench. I crouch down to follow it. Under the workbench, it's dark. There are some dusty boxes. I push a couple of them out of the way.

"Don't move things!" Tenley says.

"Sorry. Just a second . . ."

Tenley hates being down here. I should respect that. This phone thing is just too weird to let go.

I keep following the cord. Then I notice something. It seems impossible.

"Ryan! Earth to Ryan!" Tenley calls.

I look at her.

"Um . . ."

"What? Spit it out!"

"The phone," I say, clearing my throat. "It's not plugged in."

CHAPTER 6

ANOTHER GREAT IDEA

I told you not to follow the cord!" Tenley says the next day. We're walking through the halls of Scarecrow Middle School. First period starts soon. "A rat probably chewed through it. So gross!"

"That doesn't explain how the phone worked, though," I say. "Even if a rat did chew through the cord, it didn't happen *while* I was talking to that guy."

When I followed the cord yesterday, it was in two pieces. A small piece was plugged into the wall. The piece coming out of the phone wasn't plugged into anything. Wires stuck out of both pieces.

"We should try to trace the phone call."

Tenley gives me a horrified look.

"I'm serious. This whole thing is too weird not to follow up."

"That's exactly why we *shouldn't* follow up! I told you about Malay, the cursed doll. There's weird stuff in that basement. It's best to leave it alone."

21

"Look at the lovebirds!" a voice calls.

Right away, Tenley and I know who it is.

Danny walks up to us. He always wears the same gray hoodie. Most of the time, he has the hood on, even indoors. It's to cover up his bad skin rashes.

"Whatever, Danny," Tenley says. She rolls her eyes.

This guy is bigger than almost every other kid in our grade. Bullying people is his favorite thing to do. Most kids just ignore him, though.

"We're just friends," I say. "You'd know what that's like if you had any."

"Haha, loser," Danny says. Then he walks away.

"What's that guy's problem?" Tenley asks.

It seems like Danny just can't help being mean. Sometimes I feel sorry for him, but he makes it hard to be his friend.

Maybe that's the deal with the mystery man calling the unplugged phone. He can't help yelling at people.

"Let's trace the phone call," I say again. "Maybe we can find out where it's coming from. My dad said he'll do it. I told him it was a project for school."

"You told your dad?" Tenley raises her eyebrows. She looks angry.

My dad works for the phone company. He's in charge of a whole phone grid or something. Now that everyone has cell phones, I don't understand why we need a phone grid. But I guess some people still use phones like the one in the Vintage Rose basement.

"Don't worry. I made up a story. Dad said all I have to do is text him when the call comes in. We need to give him the address of the Vintage Rose. It's 6805 Legend Street, right?"

"Did you Google the address? I can't believe you, Ryan!"

"My dad says that's all he needs to trace the call. There's one other thing, though."

"What?"

"The phone has to be plugged in. It's just the way old phones work."

"No way!" Tenley says this so loudly a bunch of students look at us. "We're *not* reconnecting that old phone. What happens if you trace the call? Do you *want* to find the scary guy who called?"

"Tenley," I say in a low voice. "We answered calls on a phone that *isn't plugged in*. That doesn't interest you at all?"

"Does it interest *you* that the creepy guy wants

to get you? He's upset because you messed with his phone call. Remember?"

"What's the worst thing that can happen? We're talking about a phone call. The guy can't find us. I just want to know who he is."

CHAPTER 7

PLUGGED IN

Back in the basement, I sit on the workbench. A YouTube video plays on my phone for the seventh time. It shows how to repair the wires of an old-school phone cord. Thankfully, the video is under three minutes. That means it should be fairly easy to do.

"Almost got it," I say.

"I still think this is a waste of time," Tenley says. "What did your dad say when you asked to borrow his tools?"

"Nothing," I laugh. "I just took them without asking. What did you tell your parents we were doing down here?"

Tenley's parents are upstairs. They barely noticed us when we came in. A bunch of people were in the shop. Some were inspecting items in the pass-along section. That's a part of the store where people donate things. Then customers can take them for free.

Tenley sighs. "I told them we were still organizing.

They're leaving soon anyway. There's some antique sale they need to go to. Jay is coming to run the shop."

"Hey," I say. "Look at it this way. You're getting this phone fixed for free."

"Great. Just what I wanted. Let's make the creepy ghost phone work better."

I can't help cracking up.

"Don't forget about our deal, Ryan."

"I won't. It still doesn't make sense to me, though. Why not just put this phone back in that padlocked room? Isn't that where it came from, anyway?"

"Listen," Tenley says. I can tell she's frustrated again. "We agreed to trace the call *once*. After that, we're destroying the phone. I don't know where it came from. But opening that room is a *big deal*. Nothing goes in or out unless absolutely necessary. Got it?"

"Fine," I say.

The YouTube video plays one more time as I finish connecting the wires. Then I wrap some black electrical tape around the cord.

"Ready," I say, looking at Tenley. I plug the cord into the wall.

The phone rings immediately.

Tenley and I jump. We weren't expecting that to happen.

"Well," I say. "At least we know I fixed the cord right."

"Go on," Tenley says. "Answer it and let's get this over with."

"You sure you don't want to answer it? I need to text my dad so he can do the trace."

She rolls her eyes. Usually, Tenley is a lot more fun. This situation has put her on edge, though.

"Fine," she says. Then she picks up the phone. "Hello?"

"Hi, toots!" It's the same voice as before. "I'm home to see you!"

Tenley looks at me with wide eyes. "It's him," she mouths. I take out my phone and text my dad.

Ryan

trace the call now

"Hello? You comin' to get me? It's pouring out here!"

"Uh . . ." Tenley says. She practically throws the receiver at me. I hold it up to my ear.

I hadn't planned for this part. My goal was to get the phone connected. Then I wanted to get the man on the line. Honestly, it didn't seem like my plan would work this easily.

"Is this that kid again? You think it's funny to mess with my phone call? You got a friend there prankin' with you or something?"

Tenley hits my shoulder.

"Hang up the phone!" she whispers.

"Sir," I say. We have to keep him on the line. At least that's how tracing a call works in the movies. Maybe I should have asked my dad about it. "Uh . . . who are you trying to reach? Maybe I can help."

"Help? *Help?*"

Tenley grabs the receiver from my hand. I try to snatch it back. She's going to hang up again. If she does, the call might not be traced.

"Sir," she says into the receiver. "*You* keep calling *us*. I promise we're not who you're looking for."

"I'm going to get you two!" the man yells. "Now I mean it! You keep messin' with my call!"

Tenley slams the phone back on the cradle.

CHAPTER 8

PRANK CALL

The phone immediately rings again.

"I'm going to kill you, Ryan!" Tenley says. Then she grabs the cord. I think she's going to rip it out of the wall.

Before that happens, I pick up the phone.

"Hello?"

"I'm coming to get you, Tenley and Ryan!" a man's voice says. It's gruff, garbled, and loud. In fact, the voice is so loud that Tenley freezes when she hears it.

"Listen," I say, shaking. Suddenly, this plan I thought would be fun is now kind of scary. Maybe Tenley was right. "We're really sorry—"

"If I were you, I'd be sorry too," the man says. "Sorry for being born!"

The voice on the other end cracks up. But it doesn't sound like the man looking for Lorraine.

"You guys are too easy!" he says.

Tenley grabs the receiver and puts it to her ear.

"Jay?" she asks.

"Yeah." He continues to laugh. "What are you losers doing?"

I breathe a sigh of relief.

Jay and I don't talk much. His voice sounds completely different on the phone. He got me and Tenley good.

"We're cleaning the basement," Tenley says.

"Still? Bo-ring!" Jay laughs.

"How did you call us?" Tenley asks.

"Uh, with my phone?" Jay says. "I called the shop. Anyway, tell Mom and Dad I have practice after school. There's no way I can work today."

"Okay," Tenley says.

"And stay off the phone, Tenley! It's for business purposes *only*."

Jay starts laughing again. Then he hangs up.

"Wow," I say. "So this phone works now. And it's the same line as the shop phone."

"Not for long." Tenley moves to pull the cord out of the wall again.

Right at that moment, my cell phone rings. I look at the caller ID. It's a number I don't recognize.

CHAPTER 9

TRACED

"You want to answer it?" I ask, holding my phone up to Tenley's face.

"No!" She pushes my hand away. "It's your phone. You answer it."

I stare at the screen. Getting a call is unusual for me. Most of the time, I get texts and emails. Sometimes Tenley and I video chat. That's not the same as a phone call, though.

"Ryan, answer before it stops ringing!"

I swipe to answer the call.

"Hello?" I say nervously.

At first, all I hear is faint background noise.

"Is this Ryan Parker?" a man suddenly says. He doesn't sound like the man that's been calling us.

"Yes," I say slowly.

"My name is Allen. I work at the Scarecrow Phone Company with your father. He told me about your school project."

"Oh, hi." Relief floods my body.

My dad never calls me from his work number. He always texts from his smartphone. This is why I didn't recognize the number on the caller ID.

"We were able to trace the number to the port in Sunnyside," Allen says. "Then, for some reason, the call redirected from the residence of Lorraine Sanders to the store line. This is really unusual. Do you have a pen? I can give you both addresses when you're ready."

"Who is it?" Tenley whispers.

I hold up my hand to signal for her to wait.

"One second," I say. Then I open the notes app on my phone. There are no pens down here, but this will work to take down the addresses.

"What are you doing?" Tenley asks.

"Shh," I put my finger to my lips. Then I put Allen on speaker.

"Okay," I say. "You can give me the addresses now."

Tenley's eyes get wide. Neither of us can believe it. My plan actually worked.

CHAPTER 10

GETTING THROUGH

Tenley studies the address. "345 Happy Pilante Way," she says. "Where is that?"

I map the address on my phone. "It's in Maraab Valley. That isn't far from here. Looks like it's about halfway to Sunnyside."

Maraab Valley is a very small town. Only about 500 people live there.

Tenley and I sit in a booth at Reggie's. This is a candy and ice cream shop. It's in Scarecrow Plaza, the biggest strip mall in town. Reggie, the shop's owner, took over the store from his parents. He kept the theme of an old-time shop. The inside looks like a classic soda fountain.

We needed to get out of the Vintage Rose basement. Since it wasn't raining, we walked to Reggie's. Each of us got a scoop of ice cream. Mine is mint chip. Tenley got fudge brownie.

"I know you're stoked that the trace worked," Tenley says. "But we're still getting rid of that phone."

My heart sinks a little. Before we came to Reggie's, I convinced her not to do anything to the phone yet. The mystery is just starting to unfold.

We don't know why the man keeps calling us. He said his ship had just come in, so it makes sense that he's calling from the port. Why is the call redirecting to the store, though? Who is Lorraine Sanders? I can't stop thinking about these questions.

"Tenley," I say. "That isn't going to solve anything. It's not like getting rid of the phone will get rid of the person calling on it too!"

She gives me a look. "We'll be safer if it's gone."

"No, we won't! That guy keeps calling. He said he was going to get us. That will happen whether we have the phone or not. We may as well just keep it. Then at least we can try to figure this out."

Tenley puts a big spoonful of ice cream in her mouth. She appears to be thinking as she chews the brownie pieces.

"Next, you're going to suggest we go to Maraab Valley and find that Lorraine person." She narrows her eyes. "That's exactly what you're thinking, isn't it?

Well, no way, Ryan. *No. Way.* Don't even think about it! I mean it."

People in the shop are staring at us now. "Tenley," I say in a low voice. "That phone gets calls when it isn't even plugged in. Don't you want to find out how? What if we can find Lorraine? Or the man? Maybe we can figure out what's going on."

"Yeah, and get killed in the process."

"We're not going to get killed."

"How can you be so sure?" Tenley asks. "That man on the phone is *so* mad at us. What would we even say to him?"

"It's simple. If anything happens, we'll call the police." I hold up my phone. "Nothing's going to happen, though."

"Even if I wanted to go," Tenley says, putting another spoonful of ice cream in her mouth. "How are we going to get to Maraab Valley, anyway?"

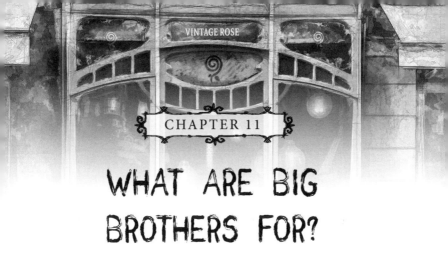

CHAPTER 11

WHAT ARE BIG BROTHERS FOR?

The next day, we're standing in Tenley's living room. It's Saturday morning.

"Drive you two nerds to Maraab Valley?" Jay says. "No way. I'd rather do homework for the next million years. Besides, I already have plans. I'm going to play a ton of *Clan Castles*. They just released all these new levels. I'm not going anywhere."

"See, Ryan," Tenley says to me. "I told you he would be too scared."

Tenley acts like she's going to walk out the front door. The floorboards creak as she moves.

This house is only a little less creepy than the Vintage Rose. It has three stories. Tenley told me that when her family first moved here, they couldn't use the third floor. Her dad's Aunt Rose had filled it with antiques. She was a major hoarder. Eventually, they moved the old junk out. Most of it ended up at the Vintage Rose.

"Me?" Jay asks. "Scared? Of what? Being bored to death by hanging out with you two losers?"

"No, don't worry about it."

Tenley swings open the house's dark purple front door. She's a really good actress. I actually believe she's going to walk out.

Jay looks at me. "What are you two up to?"

"Should we tell him, Tenley?" I ask. Now that she's gotten his attention, I can help her out. "In case something *does* happen to us."

"What do I care if something happens to you two?" Jay takes out his phone. I figure he's about to start playing *Clan Castles* any second. We have to hurry or we'll lose him to that game.

"Well," Tenley says. "Remember what happened with that doll from the shop? Malay?"

Jay looks up from his phone. His expression gets serious. I've never seen him look like that. He's always clowning around and cracking jokes.

"Tenley," he says. His tone is ice-cold. "Don't joke about that. Seriously."

"I'm not," Tenley says. "This is a similar situation."

"Does Ryan know what we're talking about?"

Tenley nods.

"Oh man," Jay says. He shakes his head. Then he actually puts his phone in his pocket. "What did you two do?"

Tenley and I tell Jay about the phone. We explain how it just appeared in the basement. Then it rang, so we picked it up. Now the person calling seems to be out to get us.

"How would he even find you?" Jay asks.

"I don't know," Tenley says. "But what if he does? And you knew about it? If he gets us, it'll be all your fault."

"Fine," Jay sighs. "I'll drive you to Maraab Valley. Once. That's it!"

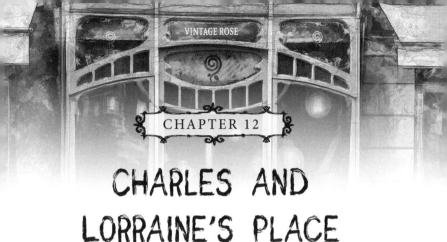

CHAPTER 12

CHARLES AND LORRAINE'S PLACE

On the way to Maraab Valley, Tenley sits up front with Jay. I sit in the back. It's a good thing I'm wearing my seat belt. Jay is driving like we're in a hurry. He sings along to the heavy metal music on the radio. The bass shakes the car. Tenley tries to turn it down, but Jay turns it back up. They keep arguing about it.

Huge, dark storm clouds hang in the sky the whole way. A few drops start to hit the windshield just as we leave Scarecrow. By the time we get to Maraab Valley, it's pouring. This must be the storm we've been hearing about.

We're using my phone to navigate. For some reason, the app is being really slow. It keeps telling us where to go at the last second. My dad made sure I got the fastest data plan. This doesn't make any sense. Maybe all the storm clouds are blocking the satellite.

I guess it could also be Maraab Valley itself. The place is a valley, after all. The road we're on slopes down steadily. Big, green trees surround us.

"If we get all the way out here and can't find it," Jay says, "you won't have to worry about the guy on the phone anymore. I'll finish what he started!"

"Don't threaten us," Tenley snaps. "I'll tell Mom and Dad."

"What would they say if I told them about this phone adventure?" Jay asks.

"We'll find it," I say.

I decide to plug the address we got into a real estate site. My mom is a real estate agent. She's always looking at these sites. Maybe I can find a photo of the house we're looking for.

After I type in the address, the site takes a few seconds to load.

Finally, it shows me 345 Happy Pilante Way in Maraab Valley. I can't believe what I'm seeing.

"This house has apparently been abandoned since the 1950s," I say.

"*Abandoned?*" Tenley asks. "Then how is somebody calling us . . ."

Her voice trails off. I know what she was going to say, though. How is somebody calling us from the house if nobody lives there? A chill runs through my body at the thought.

Soon, I'm wondering if we're even going to the right place. Did the trace give us the wrong address? Should we have tried to go to Sunnyside Port instead?

I don't say anything. Getting Jay to drive us out here was difficult enough. There's no way he'd take us all the way to the port now.

"The nav says to make your next right, Jay."

He turns down a long, winding road. Tall, green grass surrounds it on both sides. I never knew Maraab Valley was so green. Scarecrow is always overcast and gray. This place looks so lush in comparison.

Eventually, the road ends. We come to a gray two-story house. It stands out among all the green grass and trees. This house sort of looks like the one in the picture on the real estate site. But it doesn't seem abandoned. A classic white truck sits in front of it on a dirt driveway. There's a porch with wooden steps leading up to the front door.

"It feels like we've gone back in time," I mumble.

"Yeah," Tenley agrees.

Rain pounds the car furiously. We almost have to yell to hear one another now.

For a moment, we all sit there staring at the house.

Then I notice a wooden sign hanging over the front door. In big block letters, it reads "CHARLES AND LORRAINE'S PLACE."

"Lorraine," I say. "That's who the guy asked for when he called. His name must be Charles. This is the right place."

"You guys sure you want to do this?" Jay asks.

"We have to see who's in there," I say. "Otherwise, he's just going to keep calling."

"You don't know that this will stop it," Jay says.

"We don't know that it won't."

I open the car door. Tenley opens hers too.

"Hurry up!" Jay barks. "I'll keep the car running, but I don't want to burn all my gas."

"We didn't bring an umbrella, did we?" Tenley asks.

"Nope." I shrug.

We probably should have dressed warmer too. At least Tenley is wearing a hooded sweatshirt. I'm just in a T-shirt and jeans, as usual.

Tenley and I go out into the pouring rain. The air is cold too. It stings my face as we run toward the house.

Surprisingly, the outside of the house seems to be in good shape. The gray paint doesn't look faded at all. It isn't even chipping. A house this old shouldn't look so new.

Honk!

Jay blasts the car horn.

Tenley turns and glares at him. "What?"

Jay has rolled down the window to shout at us. "Move it!" He points at the house. "See if somebody's home, or let's get out of here!"

Tenley and I hurry up the wooden steps to the front door.

"You want to do it?" I ask.

"No. You do it."

Jay honks again. This guy has zero patience.

I knock on the door. My hand is so cold that it hurts my knuckles.

There's no answer.

"Maybe nobody's home?" Tenley says. She seems relieved.

I knock one more time. We both stand there. Nothing happens.

This is a bummer. We came all the way to Maraab Valley for nothing. Maybe we should have gone to Sunnyside Port after all.

Just as we are about to head back to the car, I hear a click.

The front door slowly opens.

CHAPTER 13

MISSED CALL

Behind the door is a woman in a blue dress. Her short blond hair is curled on the sides and in the back. It's a style I've only seen in old movies. There's something odd about her clothes and shoes too. They look like they came from a vintage store. She's awfully dressed up for being home on a rainy day.

"Why, hello!" The woman smiles. It's almost like she has been expecting us. "Are you lost? I don't blame you trying to get out of the rain."

She stares into the front yard. The rain is coming down harder now.

"Hi," I say. "Yes, we are hoping to get out of the rain. Are you Lorraine?" I point up at the sign above the door.

"That's me! You two want to come inside?"

I look at Tenley. She gives me a little nod.

"That would be great," I say. "Just for a moment, of course. We can't stay long."

47

Lorraine swings open the door. Tenley and I walk into the house.

The entryway leads into a large living room. There are hardwood floors. All the walls are cream-colored. Everything in the house looks completely retro. In the living room, there's a green sofa. A tall mirror leans against the wall. There's also a radio. It's wooden and rounded on top.

"Isn't it wonderful that the war is over?" Lorraine says as she shuts the door. She hasn't stopped smiling since she opened it. "My husband, Charles, made it through. I'm so relieved. Now he's on a ship, headed home."

"War?" Tenley asks. "What war?"

"What war?" Lorraine cracks up. "Why, the only war anybody's been talking about for the past five years! We beat the Germans and that evil Hitler! With the help of our great Allies, of course."

Tenley gives me a look. Is she talking about World War II? Didn't that end a really long time ago? I am so confused.

Outside, thunder booms. I glance out the window to see the rain coming down in sheets.

"This storm keeps getting worse and worse," Lorraine says. "I'm so frightful it will interrupt my phone connection. I keep checking to make sure there's a dial tone."

I smile at Lorraine. "Oh, I'm sure it's fine. Phone lines are much better than they used to be. My dad works for the phone company."

"Really? That's wonderful! I'm expecting an important call. Charles should arrive at the port very soon. He's going to call me the second he gets in. I hate to be rude, but you'll both have to leave as soon as he calls. You can have a seat and wait out the storm until then."

Tenley and I move toward the sofa. I really want to figure out what's going on. Talking to Lorraine is confusing me even more, though.

As soon as we sit down, I notice something. There's a phone on a stand next to the sofa. It looks exactly like the one in the Vintage Rose basement. Suddenly, it rings.

"That's him!" Lorraine cries. "His ship must have come in. He said he would call the minute he arrived. You'll have to go now. It was lovely meeting you! I'm sorry we couldn't chat longer."

Lorraine hurries to pick up the phone.

Tenley pokes my arm. "Hey," she hisses. "Come on. Let's go."

The two of us slip out the front door. I close it behind us.

"Ryan," Tenley says as we stand on the steps. "What just happened?"

"I . . . don't know."

"Why was Lorraine dressed that way?" Tenley goes on. "What was up with all the old stuff in her house? Does she really think World War II just ended?"

I'm not sure how to begin processing the past five minutes.

After a few seconds, I knock on the door again. There must be a way to explain all of this. We just need to talk more to Lorraine.

"What are you doing?" Tenley snaps.

The door opens before I can answer.

Lorraine stands there with a big smile on her face.

"Why, hello! Are you lost? I don't blame you trying to get out of the rain."

Tenley and I are speechless. Lorraine seems to be meeting us again for the first time. She's even saying the exact same things.

"Isn't it wonderful that the war is over?" Lorraine asks again.

Her smile was charming before. Now it seems eerie.

"My husband, Charles, made it through. I'm so relieved. Now he's on a ship, headed home."

She repeats what she told us before, word for word.

"Ma'am," I say to her. "Don't you remember meeting us? Just a few minutes ago? You invited us in. Then your phone rang—"

At that moment, the phone rings again. Lorraine rushes to get it. The door slams shut.

I raise my hand to knock again. Tenley blocks it.

"Don't," she says, glaring at me.

"But—"

Honk! Honk! Honk!

Jay honks the horn again. Lightning strikes nearby. Thunder booms. Rain pours all around us.

"We're leaving!" Tenley shouts.

She literally drags me away from Charles and Lorraine's house.

CHAPTER 14

LIVING IN THE PAST

We came all the way here for that?" Jay says. "That lady sounds senile. How else do you explain having the exact same conversation twice? She's living in the past!"

As we drive back to Scarecrow, it continues to pour. We can barely see out of the car windows. The road is wet and slick. Jay drives a lot slower than he did on the way here. He has the radio turned off too.

"I hate driving in the rain," Jay says. His hands grip the steering wheel tightly.

"That house was supposed to be abandoned," I say. "So how is Lorraine living there? It's not like she's squatting. The place seemed really nice."

"What was she talking about?" Tenley asks. "Hitler was defeated in World War II. That was decades ago. Why did she act like the war had just ended?"

"You guys got pranked," Jay says. "We never

should have gone there in the first place. I could have stayed home and played *Clan Castles*. Thanks a lot."

Tenley and I are quiet. I'm still trying to figure out what just happened.

After a few minutes, the car merges onto the highway toward home. We pass a sign that says "Welcome to Scarecrow." Something seems odd about it. I remember the sign looking faded and old. People talked about replacing it with a new electric one. Now the sign looks brand-new. Maybe the heavy rain cleaned it somehow.

We turn onto the main road into town. Jay drives past Scarecrow Plaza.

"Is there a classic car show today?" he asks.

I look out the window. A bunch of old cars are parked on the street. They are all in perfect condition. There's a classic Ford in the lane next to us too.

"Not that I know of," I say.

"Look at the signs on the stores," Tenley says. "They all look different too."

She's right. Most of the signs use skinny capital letters. Some have different logos than I remember. The electronics store sign says "Appliances" in big letters.

"Huh," I say. "It's like they're from another time." The words hang in the air. "Kind of like . . . Lorraine."

We come to a stoplight. It's right in front of Scarecrow Plaza.

Now we're close enough to read the signs on the smaller stores. What used to be the art supply store is a barber shop. A sign where the sushi restaurant was now says "Shoe Repair." There's a tailor in the spot that used to sell video games. Scarecrow Supermarket is still a grocery store, but its brown-and-white sign looks new and totally retro.

"What happened?" Tenley asks. She turns around and looks at me.

"It seems like we've gone . . . back in time," I say slowly. "But how?"

"I knew hanging out with you two was a bad idea," Jay says.

Rain continues to beat down on the roof of the car.

CHAPTER 15

NO SERVICE

Well," I say, "At least *this* place looks normal."

We are sitting in a booth at Manny's. It's in the same spot as Reggie's. So far, this is the only place that looks like we remember. That's because Reggie's had been decorated to look like an old-fashioned soda fountain.

The shop is packed with people getting ice cream, malts, and candy. The girls wear dresses and skirts. Some of them have fancy hats on too. Most of the guys wear sweaters and slacks. A few are wearing suspenders. So far, nobody seems to have noticed our jeans, T-shirts, and hoodies. I feel so out of place.

The three of us got ice cream. Normally, three cones would be close to eight dollars. Manny only charged us 30 cents!

We know who Manny is because he's wearing a name badge. He's busy scooping ice cream behind the counter. A woman helps him. Her badge says Candace.

The way they talk, I figure they are married. Both of them seem to love helping customers.

An older woman sits near the counter. She holds a baby. When the line dies down, Manny and Candace go over to them. They talk to the baby. I heard them call him Reggie.

"That's *the* Reggie," I whisper to Tenley and Jay. It's kind of exciting being able to see Scarecrow history before it happens. "He's going to take over this place!"

They both glare at me.

"Should we try to go home?" Tenley asks.

"How?" Jay says. "If it's 1945, we have no home to go to."

I didn't think about that. My house wasn't built until the 1960s.

"You're right," I mumble.

"We can't call our parents," Jay adds. "They weren't even born yet."

That gives me an idea. "We have our phones," I say. "Maybe we can look up time travel online."

I pull mine out. Jay and Tenley do the same.

My phone won't even turn on.

"Mine doesn't work, either," Tenley says. She puts hers on the table.

"They don't work," Jay says. He eyes his black screen. "I knew they wouldn't."

"Well," I say. "We can try to look on the bright side."

"What bright side?" Tenley snaps.

"Did you guys ever think we'd be time travelers?"

CHAPTER 16

BROKEN IN TIME

After finishing our ice cream, we get back in the car. Without our phones or the internet, there's only one place we can think of to go.

The Scarecrow Library is a burgundy building with lots of windows. In front, there are concrete benches hidden by big bushes. I remember mature trees surrounding the library. It's strange to see those same trees now. They're barely as tall as I am.

Inside, the library has rows of books. That hasn't changed. There are no computers to look anything up, though. Instead, there's an entire wall of tiny drawers. These are filled with index cards. People open the drawers, pull out cards, and use them to find books somehow. As a kid, I went to the library with my grandpa a lot. He used to talk about the "card catalog." I never thought I would see one in real life.

Some people work at wooden tables. Books are sprawled out in front of them. Everyone has pencils and notebooks. There's not a laptop or tablet anywhere. It's eerily quiet.

"Can I help you?" a librarian asks. She looks us up and down. I'm sure she's wondering where—or when—we came from.

I don't know if anyone can help us now, but it's worth a shot. "Uh . . . do you have any books on time travel?" I ask.

Her eyes widen. Jay and Tenley look at each other.

"Time travel theories? I think we may have a few," she says. "They're over here. Follow me."

She leads us to a shelf of dusty books. Jay pulls one out. The librarian grabs three more and hands them to me.

"Is this all?" I ask.

She nods. "Unless you want fiction?"

"No, this is fine," I tell her. "Thank you."

Tenley, Jay, and I go to the most secluded table. We each take a book and start reading. After five minutes, Jay slams his shut.

"There's no point in looking at these!" he says loudly.

"Shh," Tenley says.

"You *shh*," he snaps back. "These books are totally outdated!" A few people in the library are staring at us now. "This is simple. You two messed something up. Now we're in a different time."

"What?" I say.

"How?" Tenley asks.

"I don't know! Maybe by answering that stupid phone in the first place. Or going to that house. Why do you think that lady was so weird? She was not from our time!"

The librarian gives Jay a look from across the room.

"Sorry," he mouths to her. Then he leans in, talking in a hushed whisper. Tenley and I lean in too. "Think about it. At one point, her husband was coming home from the war. She was waiting for him to call when he got off the ship. He did . . . but somehow you guys picked up the phone!"

"The phone at the Vintage Rose," I say, putting the pieces together. "It must have been theirs. Some wires got crossed and Charles is calling it in our time . . . but he's in 1945."

"So Lorraine's not getting the call," Tenley says. "We are. She's stuck in time waiting for it."

"And *he* must be stuck at Sunnyside Port," I say. "That's why the phone company traced the call there. Charles is using a phone at the port in 1945. He's calling their house, but it's ending up at the Vintage Rose in our time."

"Yes, okay, sure," Jay says. His voice is getting louder again. "Whatever is going on, we're trapped in the past and it's all *your* fault!"

"She never got the call," I say, still trying to figure this out. "We kept answering it at the Vintage Rose. Did that mess up the timeline even more somehow?"

Tenley shrugs. "Maybe. But what do we do?"

"I don't want to be involved," Jay groans.

"You don't want to be involved?" Tenley asks. "Look around, Jay. It's 1945. You're involved!"

"Maybe this has something to do with the big storm?" I say. "One happened in 1945. A similar one was happening in our time. Could the storms have messed with the phone lines across time?"

"How could a storm make a phone ring in a different time?" Jay asks. "You guys said the phone wasn't even plugged in."

"Maybe the phone itself was cursed," Tenley says. Her body deflates a bit in her chair. "It *was* supposed to be locked up in that secret room."

"This is terrible," Jay says. "I hate history. And now I'm living in it!"

While they're talking, I glance down at the chair

next to me. Someone has left a newspaper on it. I pick it up. This might be the first time I've ever looked at one.

The headline on the front page reads "Economy Robust a Decade After War."

This doesn't make sense. Lorraine said the war just ended.

I look at the date. It says September 2, 1955.

"Guys," I say. "We're not in 1945 anymore."

CHAPTER 17

PHONE HOME

What are you talking about?" Jay asks. "That lady said World War II just ended. Even *I* know that happened in 1945."

I show them the newspaper.

"How did we jump ten years ahead?" I ask.

"Who knows," Tenley says. "None of this makes sense."

I open the newspaper just to be sure of the date. It's the same on all the pages. Then something catches my eye on the bottom corner of a page.

"Look," I say. "There's an ad in here for the Vintage Rose. Crazy!"

Tenley and Jay look at each other. Then they look at me. It's like we all have the same idea at once.

"If we can go to the Vintage Rose," Jay starts.

"Maybe we can find the cursed phone," Tenley adds.

"And if we find it," I say, "there's a chance we can get back to our time!"

The three of us scramble out of the library. Soon, we're on our way to the Vintage Rose.

"Let's say we find the phone," Jay says. He's still driving really carefully in the rain. "Then what are we going to do?"

I think for a moment. "Well . . . we have to take it back to Charles and Lorraine's place."

"What?" Tenley asks. "Why?"

"Somehow Lorraine and Charles are in alternate times. Charles's call isn't getting through to Lorraine's phone. It's going to the phone at the Vintage Rose. Hopefully, we can find that phone. Then we have to take it back to Lorraine's house and plug it in. This should allow her to get Charles's call."

"So plugging the phone in will end the time loop Lorraine is trapped in?" Tenley asks.

"Right. She's just been waiting for Charles's call. That's why she keeps reliving that moment over and over."

"There's no way this will work," Jay says. "We might as well just accept that we're stuck in 1955."

"We have to try something," I say.

"He's right," Tenley says. "And it *could* work."

"But . . ." Jay says. "Why is the call not going where it's supposed to? It makes no sense!"

"Who knows," I say. "I think this crazy storm messed something up. Somehow Charles's call got diverted to us in a different time."

"Whatever," Jay sighs. "I'm over this sci-fi stuff. This had better get us home or I'm done driving you two around for good."

A moment later, we pull up to the Vintage Rose. The shop has a corner storefront. There are four large windows. Above the front door in big, red letters, it says "Vintage Rose Antique Shop." Underneath that, a banner hangs. It says "Huge Sale!"

Jay parks a block away. We jump out of the car and run to the shop, dodging the rain.

The store is a lot more crowded than I've ever seen it. People browse the aisles of antiques. In 1955, it doesn't seem as dusty inside. The place still smells like dead roses, though.

Jay stares at the man behind the counter. His gray hair is thinning, but his mustache is jet black. He wears a button-down shirt and a black tie.

"Are you okay?" Tenley asks Jay.

"Yeah," he says. "I'm just thinking about Mom and Dad. If this plan doesn't work, we'll never see them again. Somehow we'll exist . . . without ever being born."

"Let's look for the phone," I say.

We split up. I start looking through the shelves. Everything is even older than the stuff in the Vintage Rose from our time.

Eventually, Jay and I meet in the pass-along section.

"I haven't seen it," Jay says. He seems really sad. "It's probably not here."

"What if it's in the basement?" I say. "How do we get down there?"

Jay shrugs.

"Sir!" We hear Tenley shouting. Her voice carries over all the noise. "I *need* that phone!"

Jay and I rush over to Tenley. She's talking to a tall man in a suit. He's with a short lady in a pink dress.

My eyes get wide when I see what the man is holding. It's the phone from the basement! The cord is wrapped around it. Even better, the end hasn't been cut off. A price tag on the phone says $1.25.

"I found this first," the man says. "Fair and square!"

"What if we pay you double the price for it?" I say, reaching into my pocket. Hopefully, there's some money in it.

"You'd pay double for *this?*" The man laughs. He looks at the lady next to him. She laughs too. "It's at least ten years old."

"That's perfect," Tenley says.

We stare at the phone, transfixed. This could be the key to getting us back to our time.

"How about triple?" the lady suggests.

"Fine," Jay says.

"You three have a deal," the man says, laughing. "But you know you still have to pay the shopkeeper for it."

"That's fine," I say, counting my money. I have seven dollars—more than enough! "You have no idea how important *that* phone is to me."

"To *us!*" Tenley says.

After buying the phone, we rush out of the Vintage Rose. The rain has let up a little. Just as we are about to get in the car, a man in a green Army uniform moves in front of us. He seems to have come out of nowhere. His black hair is cut short.

"Hey!" the man cries. He points to the phone Tenley's holding. "That's my phone!"

The three of us freeze in our tracks. I look at Tenley. We know this voice. It's the same one that came through the phone in the basement of the Vintage Rose.

"Are you Charles?" Tenley asks. Her eyes are wide.

"I most certainly am!" he says. His voice sounds even scarier now than it did on the phone. "It took me forever to get home after the war. You no-good kids messed with my phone call!"

"Um," Jay says. He clears his throat. "I didn't do anything, sir."

"My sweet Lorraine waited and waited for my call. Then I had to hitchhike home during this awful storm. When I finally got there, she was gone. The house was empty. I had my friend at the phone company trace where my call was going. It led me here. Where's my Lorraine? What did you kids do to that phone? Give it back. That's my property!"

Charles reaches for the phone. Tenley dodges him.

We run toward the car. Charles chases us.

"That's my phone!" he yells. "Give it back!"

CHAPTER 18

FLOATING AWAY

All of us get in the car. Jay locks the doors and starts the engine.

"Where'd he go?" Tenley asks. We look around for Charles. It's hard to see. The rain has picked up again.

"I don't see him," I say.

"Let's get out of here!" Jay says, stepping on the gas.

We pull onto one of Scarecrow's main roads. It leads out of town.

"This Charles guy is a major creeper," Jay says. "Why does he think we know what happened to Lorraine?"

"To him it's still 1945," I say. "Didn't you see? Charles is still in his uniform. He must have traveled through time just like we did."

"Charles is in love with Lorraine," Tenley says. "He'll never stop trying to find her." She stares at the phone. I think we're both half-expecting it to ring at any moment.

"I hope that phone works at their house," I say. "Maybe that will put everything right."

Honk!

The three of us jump. Tenley and I look out the back window.

A white truck is behind us. It's the same one that was in front of Charles and Lorraine's house in 1945. The headlights are so close they're blinding.

"He's following us!" Tenley screams.

Luckily, we're out of Scarecrow now. There aren't as many cars on the road. Jay speeds up. Charles drives faster too. He continues to honk. At times, his bumper nearly touches our car.

"How are we going to get the phone set up?" Jay asks. "Especially with him chasing us? He's not going to let us into his house!"

"Maybe Lorraine will?" I say. "If she's still there."

"Be careful, Jay," Tenley says. "The roads are so wet. You could lose control."

"You want me to pull over?" Jay barks.

Soon, the green trees on the outskirts of Maraab Valley surround us again. It's raining even harder here. Wind gusts make the car swerve. We can barely see the road ahead because of the storm.

Charles is not backing off.

"He's going to run us off the road!" Tenley shouts.

Just as we start going down the slope into Maraab Valley, our car suddenly slows down.

"What's happening?" I ask.

"Uh . . . I think the car is floating," Jay says. "This storm has totally flooded the roads. We're driving on water!"

Nobody says anything. Jay grips the steering wheel. He keeps his eyes on the road.

"Hey," Tenley says after a couple of minutes. She's looking out the back window. "Charles isn't behind us anymore."

"What?" Jay and I say together.

I look out the back window too. Tenley's right. Charles and his truck are gone.

"He wasn't here in 1945!" I say. "Remember? Charles was still on his ship. When he docked, he tried calling Lorraine. But she never picked up."

"So how are *we* in 1945?" Jay asks. "We weren't even born! You guys really messed us up. First, you answered that phone in the Vintage Rose. Then you made me drive here in this storm. And you talked to that woman from the past! We might be trapped here forever. How do we know the wall in Lorraine's house has the same socket? What if we get all the way there and we can't even plug in the phone?"

"Jay!" Tenley yells. "Calm down."

Finally, the road levels out. Our tires touch the pavement again.

"Well," I say. "The good news is we're no longer floating."

"And nobody is following us," Tenley says.

Jay is silent. Outside, lightning flashes and thunder booms. Rain pounds the car.

Soon, we turn down the long, winding road. We see Charles and Lorraine's house in the distance. A white truck sits out front. It looks just like before.

CHAPTER 19

HOUSE CALL

The three of us run up to the front door. I hold the phone from the Vintage Rose behind my back. Tenley knocks. There's no answer.

"What if she left?" Tenley whispers.

"The white truck's still here," I say.

"What if Charles is here now?" Jay asks.

We all look at one another.

I try knocking.

Finally, the door opens. Lorraine stands there. She looks the same as she did earlier.

"Why, hello!" She smiles. "Are you lost? I don't blame you trying to get out of the rain."

She's saying exactly what she said before.

"Yes," I say. "Can we come in, please? We're soaked."

"Why, of course," she says.

Once we're inside, Lorraine starts talking about the

war being over again. She tells us how she's waiting for Charles to call. Tenley and I smile and nod.

Right on cue, her phone rings.

"That's him!" Lorraine cries. "His ship must have come in. He said he would call the minute he arrived."

She runs to grab the phone.

"You'll have to go now," Lorraine says. "It was lovely meeting you! I'm sorry we couldn't chat longer."

Just as Lorraine is about to pick up the phone, it stops ringing.

We all stare at it. Lorraine looks at us. There's a curious expression on her face.

I'm scared. Last time, we left the house before she tried to answer the phone. Are we somehow messing with history even more now?

"Well," she finally says. "Where are my manners? Would the three of you like something to drink?"

"Sure," Jay says. "That would be great."

"I'll be right back." Lorraine walks into the kitchen.

"We're not supposed to be here," I whisper.

"I know," Tenley hisses.

"Plug in that freaky phone right now!" Jay says.

I quietly go over to Lorraine's phone and unplug it from the wall.

"Here," Tenley whispers. She takes the wrong

phone and sets it on the sofa. Then she hands me the one from the Vintage Rose.

I get on my knees and start to plug in the right phone.

"What are you doing?" Lorraine asks. I look up. She's holding a platter with three glasses on it.

"Uh," Jay says. "The phone company actually sent us. They heard you were having some problems. This big storm knocked out some lines. Luckily, these jobs are really easy. That's why they send local kids out to do them."

"Really?" Lorraine says. "I never called the phone company." She sets the drinks down on the coffee table.

I plug in the phone.

Tenley picks up the receiver. "We've got a dial tone!" She smiles.

"What have you done with my phone?" Lorraine says. She seems confused and a little suspicious now. I don't blame her. None of this makes much sense. Somehow, we have to try to set the past right, though.

"I told you I'm waiting for a very important call!"

Outside, there's a loud clap of thunder.

Tenley's face drops. She's still holding the receiver. "The dial tone is gone."

"Maybe it's a loose connection," I say. Then I push the plug harder into the wall.

Suddenly, the unplugged phone starts to ring.

All of us look at it.

"That's him!" Lorraine says again. "His ship must have come in. He said he would call the minute he arrived."

Lorraine goes to pick up the phone. She doesn't seem to notice that it's not plugged in. Jay moves between her and the sofa.

"No!" Tenley shouts. "Don't answer that! It's the wrong phone!" She drops the receiver of the phone I just plugged in and runs toward the sofa.

"But he's home!" Lorraine says. "My Charles is home to see me!"

The phone on the sofa stops ringing just as Tenley tackles it.

Knock, knock, knock! Someone pounds on the door.

"Who is that?" Tenley asks. There's panic in her voice.

"It must be Charles!" Lorraine says. "I was supposed to pick him up at Sunnyside Port. Maybe he couldn't wait to see me. He must have gotten a ride home." She walks toward the door.

"Ryan!" Jay shouts. "Get that phone working. She can't see him. It's the wrong Charles!"

The receiver is dangling off the phone stand. I pick it up and put it back on the cradle.

Immediately, it starts to ring.

Lorraine turns and looks at the phone. The knocking at the door stops.

"Let's go!" Tenley says. She's still clutching Lorraine's old phone.

The three of us run toward the door. We can hear Lorraine answer the new phone.

"Charles!" she says. Her voice is elated. "You're home! I'll come to Sunnyside Port at once. Oh darling, I can't wait to see you!"

I pull the door closed behind us just before she hangs up.

CHAPTER 20

RECONNECTED

Outside, it's no longer raining. Sunlight peers through the clouds.

"Guys, I think we did it," I say.

Tenley and Jay look at each other. There's the hint of a smile on Jay's face.

"So what year are we in now?" he asks as we walk down the steps.

"Look," Tenley says. She has turned around to face Charles and Lorraine's place. "It's changed."

Jay and I look back at the house. Most of the paint has chipped off. Shingles are missing from the roof. Some windows are broken. From what we can see, there's nothing inside. The house looks abandoned, just like that website said.

"Come on," Jay says. "Let's get out of here before you two mess anything else up."

Tenley and I follow Jay to the car. We all get in. Jay

turns on his loud music and speeds away. For the first time today, everything seems normal.

Soon, we're back in Scarecrow. Our town looks normal too. All the shops we remember are at Scarecrow Plaza. The signs look familiar. There are no classic cars around. Reggie's is Reggie's, not Manny's.

All of us are relieved. There's one thing we still need to do, though.

Jay drives to the Vintage Rose. We park and get out. Tenley hesitates before opening the door to the shop. I think she's afraid her parents won't be here.

"Hey, kids," her mom says as we walk in. The scent of dead roses fills my nostrils. "What have you been up to?"

"Hi, Mom," Jay grins. He goes behind the counter and gives his mom a hug. I don't think I've ever seen Jay hug his mom before.

While he does that, Tenley grabs the key ring that hangs behind the counter.

"Mom, Ryan forgot something in the basement," she says. "We need to get it really quick."

The three of us go downstairs.

"Are you guys ready?" Tenley asks.

Jay and I nod.

Tenley pulls back the black curtain with white symbols on it. She takes a deep breath. Then she unlocks the padlock. Carefully, Jay opens the door.

While Jay and I stand guard, Tenley enters the secret room. She sets the phone down and dashes back out. Jay slams the door shut, and they quickly replace the lock. Finally, Tenley pulls the black curtain back over the door.

"How do we know for sure that this will fix everything?" Jay asks. "All that back-and-forth could have messed with history or something."

"Who knows?" I say. "We just time-traveled to plug in a phone. A phone that was ringing here when it wasn't plugged in. It seems to me history was already screwed up. All we did was fix it."

"I'm just glad things seem back to normal," Tenley says. She heads upstairs. Jay and I follow her. "At least we know the phone will be safe in there. Nobody can mess with it anymore."

Upstairs, some people browse in the shop. Tenley's parents work behind the counter.

Then we hear a phone ring. It sounds just like Lorraine's phone.

Tenley, Jay, and I exchange looks. A lump rises in my throat.

"After all that?" Tenley groans. "That phone is *still* ringing?"

"What are we going to do?" I say.

"Hello?" Tenley's dad answers his smartphone. He walks toward the shop office. As he passes by us, he puts his hand over the microphone.

"Hey, guys!" he whispers to us. "Is my old-school ringtone cool or what?"

VINTAGE ROSE

VINTAGE ROSE

VINTAGE R🌀SE
MYSTERIES

CALL WAITING
9781680217629

CARNIVAL OF FEAR
9781638890478

LUCKY ME
9781680217599

NEW PAINTING
9781680217612

THE SECRET ROOM
9781680217582

VCR FROM BEYOND
9781680217605

WWW.SDLBACK.COM/VINTAGE-ROSE-MYSTERIES